FUNNY BOY

meets the AIRSICK ALIEN from ANDROMEDA

FUNNY BOY meets the AIRSICK ALIEN from ANDROMEDA

Dan Gutman

Illustrated by
John Dykes

L. A. F. :)
Books

Hyperion Books
for Children
New York

To Sam—*my* funny boy
—D.G.

For Jeffrey and Gregory,
and our friend Andrew D.
—J.D.

First Edition
3 5 7 9 10 8 6 4 2
Printed in the United States of America.

Library of Congress Cataloging-in-Publication Data
Gutman, Dan.
Funny Boy meets the airsick alien from Andromeda/Dan Gutman.—1st ed.
p. cm.
Summary: Funny Boy, a superhero who disarms villains
with his powerful sense of humor, is summoned to save Earth from
a planet-gobbling alien from outer space.
ISBN: 0-7868-1330-X (pbk.)
[1. Extraterrestrial beings—Fiction. 2. Heroes—Fiction. 3. Wit and
humor—Fiction. 4. Humorous stories.] I. Title.
PZ7.G9846   1999
[Fic]—dc21   98-43837

CONTENTS

WARNING: The story you are about to read is fictional. That means I made the whole thing up. If any of the characters in this book claim that they are real, they're lying. This story is also extremely far-fetched and silly. If there is anything in this book that you find illogical or personally offensive, consult your physician immediately and ask about getting a sense of humor transplant.

Introduction

DO YOUR JOB AND KEEP
YOUR MOUTH SHUT

Good day, Earthlings! I am Funny Boy, defender of all that is good, enemy of all that is evil. I have come to save your pathetic planet from destruction.

For years, your scientists have wasted their time arguing about whether or not there is life on other planets. Well, I am here to tell you the truth. Not only is there life on other planets, but the universe is *filled* with alien sleazeballs who would like nothing better than to destroy Earth for the pure fun of watching it explode into a zillion pieces.

Your planet needs help badly. That is why I am here.

My mission—to use the power of jokes, quips, puns, wisecracks, amusing anecdotes, and other forms of humor to fight the forces of badness and evil and wickedness.

To make a long story short, I have come to save your butt.

But I will need your help. I am but one lonely superhero and there is only so much I can do on my own. It is up to *you* to help me. Are you prepared to do your part? I will reveal your mission on the next page.

Turn the page!

That's right. Your mission is to turn the page. Here's how we will work together . . .

Start reading each page from the top line. Read all the words on the page. Then, when you reach the last word at the bottom of the page . . . *turn the page*.

Think you can handle that? Good. I knew I could count on you.

So, in case you skipped the beginning of this book (or you simply haven't been paying attention). . .

I will fight the forces of evil.

You will turn the pages.

Together, we can save Earth from the unspeakable, repulsive creep from outer space you will meet on these pages. Got it? Good. Now do your job.

—Funny Boy

Chapter 1

A PLANET THE SIZE
OF URANUS

"Knock, knock."
"Who's there?"
"Mickey Mouse's underwear."

That was the first joke I ever heard. I was three years old at the time. That's three *Earth* years, of course. On my home planet, a year only lasts one day. So I was actually 1,095 years old when I heard the Mickey Mouse joke. I am 3,287 years old now, or nine Earth years.

I was born on Crouton, which is a planet about the size of Uranus. It is the only place in the universe where anyone can say the word "Uranus" without giggling.

Crouton is shaped much like a loaf of bread. In fact, the planet is made entirely of bread. That, of course, is why it came to be called Crouton.

My people—the Croutonians—are gentle folk. Perhaps you've heard the Croutonian national anthem. It sounds like a bunch of pots and pans being banged with a wooden spoon and then thrown down a flight of stairs.

Crouton is 160,000 million light-years from Earth, in the Magellanic Clouds galaxy. It's just a stone's throw from Tinkle Major. That is, if you can throw a stone ten million miles.

For those of you who don't know what a light-year is, it's the distance light travels in one year. A light-year is very difficult to measure. That's because whenever they try to measure a light year, the batteries in the flashlight run out before the year is up and they have to start all over again.

In scientific terms, a light-year is really, really, *really* far away. It is farther than the longest, most boring car trip you have ever taken. It's so far, you could say "Are we there yet?" six *billion* times in a row, and you *still* wouldn't be there yet.

It's so far, that if you traveled from Earth to

Crouton, the trip would take an entire lifetime. And then, when you finally arrived on Crouton, you would see that there isn't much going on and you would want to come back home. It's sort of like a trip to Canada.

Crouton is very much like Earth, but quite different in some ways, too. For instance, on Crouton golf balls don't have dimples. They have pimples. On Earth, you drive on the parkway and park on the driveway. But on Crouton, we drive on the sidewalk and park in the swimming pool.

Also, Croutonian cows have thirteen udders and each one gives a different variety of soft drink.

Other than those minor differences, the two planets are pretty much the same.

Croutonians are very lazy people. Let me give you an example. My father was a volcano chaser. Not a tornado chaser. Not a hurricane chaser. He would chase volcanoes. It's much easier, because they don't move all over the place the way tornadoes and hurricanes do. Once you catch a volcano, it pretty much stays put. My dad would chase a volcano until he caught it, then he'd pull up a lawn chair and sit there watching it.

My mother was pretty average. She was a stay-at-home mom for five years, until the day my dad talked her into going outside. By the time my brother and I were in school, Mom started her own company making finger puppets for people with extremely large hands. In her spare time she would get together with the ladies in her bridge club, and they built some really nice ones.

My brother—his name is Bronk—and I always had a normal relationship. I hated his guts and he hated mine. Once, as a practical joke, he put

chlorine from our swimming pool into my oat-
meal. To pay him back, I put darts on the blades
of the ceiling fan over his bed and programmed it
to turn on when his alarm clock went off in the
morning. Mom grounded both of us for a week.

We also have a dog, a cocker spaniel named
Punchline, who doesn't do much more than bark
all day. More on her later.

All in all, I had a typical, happy, carefree childhood on the planet Crouton. And then one day,
something terrible happened.

PLANETARY PROFILE OF CROUTON

Population: Yes, there are people there.

Geography: The mountainous regions are quite low and flat, while the lowlands are elevated and very steep.

Capital: Yes, and we have small letters, too.

Industries: We manufacture bubble wrap paper, zippers, snorkels, novelty T-shirts, automobile air fresheners, meat thermometers, and those stupid plastic CD cases that are so hard to open.

Agriculture: Every day we grow more disgusted than the day before.

Currency: The blang. One blang equals fifteen hundred kleegmores.

State bird: The hippopotamus. There are no birds on Crouton, and we had to pick something.

State flag: An enormous piece of toast hanging off a flagpole.

State sport: Those wooden paddles with a rubber ball attached to an elastic string, whatever they're called.

Religion: We worship a big orange melon that some lady thinks looks like Elvis Presley's head.

State motto: "If it's yellow, let it mellow. If it's brown, flush it down."

Chapter 2

HOW TO BE SO ANNOYING THAT YOUR PARENTS SHOOT YOU INTO OUTER SPACE IN A ROCKET

You're probably wondering how I became Funny Boy.

Funny you should ask.

It all started when I was a little kid back on the planet Crouton. Everybody always thought I was funny. When I fell down while learning how to walk, everybody thought it was funny. When I was learning how to use a spoon and the food fell out of my mouth and dribbled down my face, everybody thought it was funny. When I fell off a cliff into an active volcano filled with molten lava, everybody thought it was hysterical.

Okay, I made that last one up. But the point is,

no matter what I did, people always thought it was funny. I discovered very early that I had this unusual talent to make people laugh.

It didn't take long to discover that I could use this talent to my advantage. For instance, one day for the fun of it I called up my dad's boss and told him my father had stolen a million blangs from the company. My dad was furious when he found out. But I guess he thought it over and realized how funny it was, because he was hardly mad at all when he got out of jail three months later.

Another time I was in art class at school and this bully started bothering me. I told him to leave me alone.

"Make me," he challenged.

So I took a piece of clay and built a statue that looked just like him.

"There," I said, as I presented the statue to him. "I made you."

The bully started laughing at me and never bothered me again.

I discovered something that has stayed with me my entire life—while people are laughing at me, they usually don't do mean things to me. So I figured that if I could keep people laughing at me, fewer mean things would happen.

On Crouton, I was a bit of a smart aleck, I must admit. My favorite thing to do was to play the "Why" game. Did you ever play this game with your parents?

It's simple. These are the rules: anytime anybody says anything, you just reply, "Why?"

So, for example, if your mom asks you to tie your shoes, you say, "Why?"

"So you won't trip and fall."

"Why?"

"Because you might get hurt."

"Why?"

"Because a part of your body will hit the ground hard."

"Why?"

"Because of gravity."

"Why?"

See what I mean? You could go on forever like that. The "Why" game is one of the most annoying things kids can do to grown-ups. It ranks right up there with the "I'll Repeat Everything You Say Right After You Say It" game.

As you might imagine, I was pretty annoying. One day at breakfast, when my mom wasn't looking, I shot a spitball at my brother Bronk for the fun of it. He kicked me under the table. So I shot another spitball at him. Nailed him right in the forehead. So he told on me.

"I didn't do anything!" I lied. I made sure to start whistling, because people who are innocent always whistle.

"You shoot one more spitball at your brother," Mom said, "and I'm going to put you in a rocket and send you to Earth!"

"*Earth?!*" I shuddered with horror. "*No, please! Anything but that! I'll do whatever you say! Just don't send me to Earth!*"

You see, at Croutonian schools they teach kids about all the other planets, including Earth. It sounded like an awful place. My science book said that on Earth, kids have to straighten up their rooms and make their own beds.

Is that dumb or what? On Crouton, kids don't have to straighten up their rooms. Their rooms aren't crooked. And you don't have to make your own bed, either. You just go to a store and *buy* a bed.

I learned that in Earth schools, kids have to fold their hands and sit on the floor like a pretzel. I tried to fold my hands once. I tried really hard. But they *just wouldn't fold*.

I tried to sit like a pretzel, too. It was impossible, and it took me a week to get all the salt out of my ears.

On Earth, I learned, people go on vacation and take lots of pictures. How horrible! If Earth people ever came to Crouton for a vacation, I would hide all my pictures so nobody could take them.

That's the trouble with Croutonians—they're way too literal.

Earth sounded like a terrible place to me. When Croutonian parents get mad at their kids, they always threaten to send them to Earth.

Still, I never really believed half that stuff they

told us about Earth. I never thought my parents would actually send me there, either. So I did what any other normal Croutonian kid would do.

I shot another spitball at Bronk.

The next thing I knew, I was strapped into a rocket on a launching pad.

10, 9, 8, 7 . . .

My parents were doing the countdown.

. . . 6, 5, 4, 3 . . .

Through the window of the rocket, I saw Bronk. He had his finger on the launch button. And an evil smirk on his face.

. . . 2, 1—Liftoff!

The force of the rocket taking off pushed my body against the seat so hard, my cheeks were flapping like a flag on a windy day. I felt like my flesh was going to fly off.

As you can tell, Croutonian parents are pretty strict. **When Earth kids misbehave, you might get sent to your room. My parents sent me to another *planet*.**

Still, Mom and Dad really loved me. They put my dog, Punchline, in the rocket with me to keep

me company. That would have been great, but I never really liked Punch.

To protect us during our flight to Earth, Mom and Dad packed the rocket with croutons. They were supposed to absorb the impact when the rocket landed, sort of like those Styrofoam peanuts you use to send packages that you don't want damaged in the mail.

As Punch and I entered Earth's atmosphere, I looked out the small window of the rocket. We were heading directly for a building about the size of a football field. The rocket must have been going at least three hundred miles per hour.

"This is it, Punch," I said seconds before we hit the roof. "It was nice knowing you."

**I was sure
we
were about
to
die.**

Chapter 3

A LIFETIME SUPPLY
OF UNDERWEAR

As luck would have it, there was a glass skylight in the roof. Our rocket smashed through the skylight and mysteriously began slowing down. It was as if we put on the brakes.

Finally, the rocket stopped with a gentle bump. It felt like I had landed on a soft pillow. There was no explosion, no fire. Punch and I were alive.

I looked out the window. Everything was white.

Snow, I figured immediately. We had crashed into a building filled with soft snow!

No, that didn't make sense. Why would they put snow inside a building? *How* could they put

snow inside a building? I looked more closely at the window.

Underwear!

A lifetime supply of it. We had crashed into an underwear factory, and landed on tons of cotton boxers, briefs, and panties. Of all the places to land, we hit one of the softest things on Earth.

What were the chances of that, huh?

When somebody comes to another planet, he usually has superpowers, right? When Superman arrived from Krypton, he knew right away he could do things humans couldn't do. He had super vision and super hearing. He could leap tall buildings in a single bound. He could stop bullets. He could bend steel with his bare hands. He could always find a pay phone booth that wasn't in use.

Well, when I arrived from Crouton, I expected to have some superpowers, too. But nothing was different. I wasn't extra-strong or anything. In fact, I hurt my hand pounding on the door of the rocket trying to get it open.

"Nice move, brainless!" a voice suddenly said. "Now we'll *never* get out of here."

I turned around. There was nobody in the rocket besides Punchline and me.

"Who said that?" I asked.

"Who do you think, moron?" Punch replied.

"You . . . can talk?"

"Apparently so," Punch said, looking quite pleased with herself.

This wasn't fair! Something about Earth's atmosphere had given Punch the ability to speak, but I didn't have any superpowers at all. What a rip-off!

"Now that your hand is possibly broken," Punch said, "do you have any *other* brilliant ideas to get us out of here?"

"You could try barking," I suggested.

"Sorry," Punch said, turning up her nose at

the suggestion. "I don't bark anymore."

"Help! Help!" I hollered, pounding the walls. "Let us out!"

"Why are you so uptight?" Punch asked calmly. "This isn't the real world. We're just fictional characters in some book."

"Huh?"

"You and me," she explained. "We're not real. We're fictional. It's only a book that kids will read."

"It is *not*!" I exclaimed. "It's real! If we were fictional characters, my hand wouldn't hurt so much, now would it?" I had her there.

> Does it still hurt if the dog that bites you is fictional?

"Believe whatever you want," Punch said, leaning back and putting her paws behind her head. "I'm not worried. We'll be rescued soon. Wait and see. Fictional stories always have a happy ending."

Punch had only been talking for a minute, and I was already sick of listening to her.

After about a half hour of yelling, I heard a noise outside the rocket. Somebody was digging through the underwear.

"I told you we'd be rescued," Punch said. "It never fails."

Finally, the door to the rocket creaked open. A man's face peered inside.

"Holy cow!" he said. "Now I've seen everything."

The man was wearing a white uniform with a name tag on it that read "Foster." He had brown skin, much darker than mine. I had never seen anyone with dark skin before.

"Are you tan from the sun?" I asked the man.

"No, I'm Bob, from Earth."

Earth!

All my life I had heard about Earth, with its vast continents, its abundance of living creatures, its . . . underwear. And now I was actually there. I was so excited, I forgot how envious I was that Punch had a special power and I didn't.

"Do all Earthlings spell their names the same way forward and backward, Bob?" I asked excitedly.

"No," he laughed, "just a few of us."

"You must be a very important Earthling," I said, impressed. "But Bob, how do you know if you're spelling your name right? I mean, if you spell it B-O-B, how do you know it shouldn't have been B-O-B with the two Bs reversed?"

"Are you for real?" Bob asked.

"No," Punch replied. "We're fictional."

Bob staggered backward a few steps and looked at Punch, his eyes open wide.

"D-did that dog just say something?" Bob asked.

"Unfortunately, yes," I replied as Bob helped us out of the ship. "She seems to have developed that ability as we entered Earth's atmosphere. Now she won't shut up."

There was underwear as far as the eye could see. "Why do Earthlings need so much underwear?" I asked.

"We change our underwear every day," Bob replied.

"Change it into what?" I asked, but Bob just shook his head and laughed.

He carried us down the mountain of underwear. As he placed us on the floor, Bob asked me where I came from.

"My dog Punch and I are from the planet

Crouton," I explained. "It is in the Magellanic Clouds galaxy."

He stared at us for a while with his hands on his hips.

"Are you putting me on?" he asked.

"How could I put you on?" I replied. "You're not clothes."

Bob stared at us a while longer before asking, "Why are you here?"

"It's a long story," Punch replied. "If you want

Turn left here to get to page 4.

to hear it, go back to page four and start reading. We'll wait here for you."

"Page four?" Bob asked. "What are you talking about?"

"You see, we're all part of a book," Punch continued. "Kids are going to read this. If you go back a few pages, you can learn how we came from the planet Crouton."

"Maybe *you're* part of a book, doggie," Bob declared. "I'm real."

"Oh no, you just *think* you're real," Punch told Bob. "You're just words on a page. A fictional character like us. We came from the planet Crouton, which is fictional, too."

"Crouton?" Bob looked at us with an amused expression on his face. "You mean like those little chunks of toasted bread they put on salads? That's a dumb name for a planet."

Croutonians are very proud and patriotic people. We don't like others making fun of our planet.

"Hey, what kind of name is *Earth*?" Punch asked Bob. "*Your* planet was named after dirt!"

26

We could have argued over which planet had the dumbest name, but a loud whistle suddenly blew. The workers in the underwear factory began scurrying in every direction.

"Quittin' time," Bob said, waving good-bye to us. "Enjoy your stay on Earth, you two!"

I didn't know where to go. When Superman arrived on Earth, Ma and Pa Kent discovered his rocket and they became his foster parents. I would need a foster family, too.

"Wait!" I shouted after Bob as he walked out the front gate of the underwear factory.

"Huh?" he said, turning around.

"Can my dog and I come live with you, Bob?"

"Pleeeeeease . . ." begged Punch.

"What are you, nuts?" Bob said. "Of course you can't come live with me."

"But you found us. You're my foster dad."

"What are you talking about!?"

"It says so right there," I said, pointing at the word Foster on his uniform.

"Foster is just my *name*," he insisted. "Bob Foster. I'm not your foster father."

27

"Anything you say, Dad."

Punch and I followed Bob to his car. As he got into the driver's side, Punch and I climbed up on the roof. When Bob turned the engine on, I hung my head down over the windshield and shouted, "Take me home, Daddy!"

"Go away!" Bob shouted. He put the car into gear and started zigzagging around the parking lot, trying to throw us off the roof. But Punch

28

and I were holding on pretty tightly. Finally, Bob stopped the car and got out.

"If you don't take us home with you," I informed him, "I will hold my breath until I turn blue."

(The "hold my breath until I turn blue" trick never worked back home on Crouton, but I figured it might be worth a try on Earth.)

"See if I care," Bob replied.

I noticed something on the front seat of Bob's car. It was a newspaper called the *National Inspirer*. There was a huge headline across the top of the first page:

Space Aliens Are Coming!

Below that, it said the *National Inspirer* would pay a million dollars to anyone who captured a real live space alien.

Bob glanced at the newspaper too. Then he looked at me and Punch.

"Are you and your dog *really* from another planet?" he asked.

"That's what I've been trying to tell you, Bob."

"Get in the car," Bob said.

Chapter 4

WHY DO THEY CALL IT FAST FOOD IF IT JUST SITS THERE?

As soon as we got to Bob's house, he rushed inside and started frantically dialing the telephone.

"I hope you're ordering a pizza," Punch said. "I'm starved."

"Grab something from the kitchen. I'm calling the *National Inspirer*," Bob explained excitedly. "When they see I've got real space aliens right here in my house, they'll pay me a million bucks! And then I'll never have to look at another pair of underwear again!"

Punch and I shrugged, and went into the kitchen. On the counter was a box of something called Fruit Roll-Ups. Fascinating. Instead of sim-

ply eating a piece of fresh fruit, you Earthlings apparently take the trouble to crush the fruit, dry it out, and peel it off a piece of waxed paper. Punch and I ate a dozen each. Then we ate some gummi bears, which, we discovered, were not made from real bears or real gum, either.

Bob got through to the *National Inspirer* on the phone. He started telling somebody that an alien had crash-landed into the underwear factory and was in his kitchen with a talking dog. A few seconds later, he hung up angrily.

"What did they say?" I asked.

"They said I was a nutcase."

Bob dialed the phone again. When he got through this time, he immediately said he qualified for the million-dollar reward because he had an alien in his house and could prove it.

"Here, you can talk with the alien yourself," Bob said into the phone. Then he handed it to me.

"I am from the planet Crouton," I explained. "It's about the size of Uranus—"

Click. They hung up.

"Did I say something wrong?" I asked Bob.

Bob made several more calls, but was unable to convince anyone at the *National Inspirer* that Punch and I were genuine aliens. Every time he tried, they just laughed and said rude things to him. Earthlings, I discovered, like to *believe* in aliens, but don't actually want them to exist.

I felt bad for Bob. Here he was, nice enough to take us home with him. And he couldn't even convince the *National Inspirer* that we were really aliens so he could collect the reward. Bob was really mad.

We were still hungry, so Bob took us out to what he called a "fast food" restaurant. This, I didn't understand at all. The food didn't seem very fast to me. In fact, it just sat on the tray without moving at all. Punch had to stay in the car, but we promised to bring her some food.

"How much ham is in the ham-burger?" I asked Bob.

"None," Bob informed me.

"Well, what kind of dog is in the hot dog?"

Even talking dogs have to stay in the car?

"They don't use dogs! That would be disgusting."

"So why are they called hamburgers and hot dogs?" I asked.

"Just eat," Bob said. "It's good for you."

"Did the french fries come from France?" I asked.

"No," Bob said, getting annoyed. "Have a chicken nugget. They have chicken in them, I think. They're good for you."

I looked at the nugget and tried to figure out

which part of the chicken it came from. I had seen pictures of chickens, and none of them looked even remotely like a nugget. Against my better judgment, I ate it, along with the hamburger and hot dog.

Bob offered me a soda, which at least said what was in it right on the can: carbonated water, high fructose corn syrup and/or sugar, caramel color, phosphoric acid, caffeine, citric acid, and natural flavors.

Phosphoric acid is my favorite food!

"Now *this* is good for you," I said happily. "See? It's got natural flavors."

On the way out, I stopped off to thank the lady at the cash register who took our order.

"My compliments to the chef!" I told her. "He must have labored for hours preparing this sumptuous feast."

She started laughing at me and asked, "What planet are you from, Mac?"

"I live on Crouton."

"Sorry, we don't have any croutons," she said. "You want a packet of ketchup?"

I examined the packet she handed me.

"Wow," I gushed. "This must be my lucky day! There's enough ketchup in here for another french fry!"

Bob and all the ladies working behind the counter must have thought I had a great sense of humor, because they kept laughing at me no matter what I said or did.

"You know," Bob said as we got back in the car. **"You're starting to grow on me."**

"Like a fungus?" I asked.

"No," Bob replied. "What I mean is, you and your dog can stay at my place tonight if you want to."

When the sun had set at the end of the day, Bob said it was time to go to sleep. He got some sheets, covers, and pillows out of the closet and handed them to me.

"I'll need a hammer and nails, too," I told him.

"What for?"

"So I can make my bed," I explained. "Aren't Earthlings supposed to make their beds?"

"You're funny, boy," Bob said with a yawn. "I gotta hit the sack."

"I thought you were going to sleep," I said, puzzled. "It's kind of late to be hitting a sack. And why would you want to hit a sack anyway? What did the sack ever do to you?"

"Good night."

"Good night, Dad."

Chapter 5

HOW TO USE DUMB JOKES, BAD PUNS, AND CHEAP LAUGHS TO FIGHT THE FORCES OF EVIL

The next day, when he got home from work at the underwear factory, Bob called the *National Inspirer* again. He kept trying to convince them I was from another planet so he could collect the million-dollar reward. But everybody just said he was crazy. After a while the telephone operator at the *National Inspirer* recognized his voice and hung up on him whenever he'd call.

Meanwhile, Punch and I made Bob's house our headquarters on Earth. I did Bob's laundry and cleaned the place up for him while he worked at the underwear factory.

Mostly, I watched TV. There is no TV on Crouton, so I found it fascinating. Television was like a window to the world. That is, if you looked out the window and saw car chases, explosions, houses burning down, angry people screaming at each other, and the police leading people to jail.

After watching these things on TV for a week, I became disgusted by the stupidity of it all. So I watched TV for another week just to see if it could possibly get any stupider. It did, and so did I. I felt my brain cells disintegrating more with every hour I watched. Finally, I was about to turn off the set when a public service announcement came on the screen . . .

"My name is Ryan McCaffrey of Channel 4 News. If you see a crime in progress, don't just sit there and do nothing. You can help! Channel 4 is interested in car chases, explosions, houses burning down, angry people screaming at each other, and the police leading people to jail. It is our duty to bring these things into your living room. So if you witness a crime, call us. Call the police. Call somebody, for heaven's sake! It's your responsibility as a law-abiding American."

"He's right!" I exclaimed. "I've got to do my part!"

At that moment I looked out Bob's window and I noticed an old lady with a cane crossing the street. I rushed over to do my duty as a citizen.

"Halt, elderly jaywalker!" I hollered. "Put your hands in the air and drop your weapon."

"What weapon?" she asked.

"That cane," I explained. "I saw you try to hit me with it."

"But you told me to put my hands in the air!"

"Quiet, lawbreaker!" I announced. "You have the right to remain silent. Anything you say may be used against you in a court of law."

"Leave me alone, you creep!" the lady shouted. "I've never broken the law in my life."

"You've got a lot of hostility, lady," I said. "Maybe if I told you a joke, you would not be so angry. **What lies shaking at the bottom of the ocean?**"

"What?"

"A nervous wreck," I said.

"That's stupid," the old lady said as she started walking away. "And so are you."

"Well, since this is your first offense, I'll let you go this time," I told her. "But if I catch you jaywalking again, you'll get the couch."

"The couch?" she asked, turning around. "Do you mean I'll get the chair?"

"That's right, lady," I said. "You'll get the chair *and* the couch. It will be curtains for you, too. In fact, I may have to give you an entire living room set."

"You're a moron," she said, laughing as she walked away.

Just like back home, Earth people seemed to think I was funny. In fact, they laughed at me even *more* than Croutonians. Slowly, I began to suspect that I *did* have a superpower after all. Something about the atmosphere here made me even funnier than I was back on Crouton.

On Earth, everything I did was funny. Bob said I looked funny. He said I walked funny. After a few days on Earth, he told me I smelled funny, and told me I should take a shower. Then, after I took the shower, he made me give it back.

"You are funny, boy," Bob said as he

reinstalled the shower in the bathroom. "You ought to be a comedian."

I considered it. After Punch and I had been on Earth for a few weeks, I was getting tired of sitting around Bob's house doing chores and watching television. Perhaps I could become a famous comedian and Earth people would watch *me* on television.

But I wanted to do more than simply make people laugh. I had already developed a fondness for my adopted planet. I wanted to do something that would serve the people here.

I couldn't see through walls. I couldn't stop bullets. I couldn't fly, and I had no super strength. When I punched something, it didn't go flying. I tried to kick a big rock once. I almost broke my foot.

I didn't have any of the usual superpowers, but no matter what I did, people laughed. *This* was my superpower, I realized. I could use my enhanced sense of humor to fight evil and injustice, to promote goodness and niceness throughout the world.

"You are funny, boy," Bob kept telling me.

That's when it hit me. *Funny Boy!* I had found my name. I took the yellow tablecloth off Bob's kitchen table and made it into a superhero cape. I looked at myself in the mirror and liked what I saw. But something still wasn't right. I needed to disguise myself even more. I grabbed Bob's fake nose and glasses and put them on. Perfect! I was ready. I had found my cause in life.

Chapter 6

FUNNY BOY VERSUS
THE LIBRARY LOONY

"What's with the tablecloth?" Punch asked when she saw me the next morning.

"It's not a tablecloth," I replied. "It's a cape."

"You can't fly. What do you need a cape for?"

"All superheroes have capes."

"Capes are stupid."

"They are not."

"Take my advice. Lose the cape."

"I like the cape. What do you know? You're a dog," I said. "Now it's time to go searching for bad guys so I can rid the world of them."

After I finished doing Bob's housework for the day, Punch and I patrolled the streets. We patrolled the East Side. We patrolled the West Side. We patrolled all around the town. We

couldn't find any bad guys anywhere. There were lots of bad guys on TV, but hardly any in the real world.

After a few days of this, I began to feel depressed. How could we rid the world of bad guys if there were no bad guys to rid the world of? Without bad guys there was no need for a Funny Boy, just as without cavities there is no need for dentists.

It got me thinking. Without diseases, there would be no need for doctors or hospitals. Without traffic accidents, there would be no need for auto repair shops. Without bad breath, there would be no need for Tic-Tacs. So thank goodness for cavities, diseases, traffic accidents, and bad breath. That thought made me even more depressed.

Then one day, I saw a big commotion outside the public library. Punch and I dashed over. I asked a lady what was going on.

"Some lunatic is holding up the library!" she said excitedly.

"He must be very strong to hold up a library," I marveled.

"He's *robbing* it," she said, looking at me as if I was from another planet, which I was. "The lunatic is robbing the library!"

"Why would he do that?" I asked. "Isn't the library free?"

"That's why he's a lunatic!" the woman shouted.

I rushed into the library, pushing my way through the crowd to get to the checkout desk.

The lunatic robber was pointing a water gun at the librarian.

"Give me all the overdue book money or I start squirting," the robber said.

The librarian quickly emptied her drawer, nervously putting three nickels, a dime, and some pennies on the counter. The robber scooped up the money and was about to make his getaway when I leaped into his path.

"Halt, evildoer!" I hollered. "It is I, Funny Boy!

Give back the overdue book money or I will be forced to tell jokes until you see the folly of your ways!"

"You gotta be kidding." He giggled.

"I *am* kidding," I replied. "Tell me, what did the hat say to the hat rack?"

"I give up, what did the hat say to the hat rack?"

"You stay here, I'll go on ahead."

"That's so stupid it's almost funny," the robber said with a sneer. Already, he seemed like less of a threat to society.

"Did you hear about the carpenter who left work early?" I asked him.

"What about him?" the robber replied.

"He made a bolt for the door."

"That's dumb," he said. "Did anyone ever tell you you're a moron?"

"Plenty of times," I replied. "But it will never stop me from fulfilling my goal of ridding the world of evildoers."

"You need help, pal."

"Never mind that," I continued. "What's green and has four wheels?"

"I give up."

"Grass!" I proclaimed.

"Grass doesn't have four wheels," protested the robber.

"I know," I said. "I added that part to make it harder."

"Man, I don't have time for this," the robber said, tossing the coins back on the librarian's desk and leaving. "I've got a life."

"Admit it, evildoer!" I shouted after him. "You are defenseless against my superior sense of humor!"

"You're pathetic!" he shouted as he ran away.

A siren wailed outside and some doctors wearing white lab coats rushed into the library. Quickly, they surrounded me.

"Come with us, clown man," they told me, "and nobody will get hurt."

"I am not clown man," I explained. "I am Funny Boy! I have just prevented this evildoer from robbing the library."

It took a while, but finally I was able to convince the police that I wasn't crazy.

"Thank you, Funny Boy," said a little boy

outside the library. "You're my hero!"

At least some people appreciated my talents.

A few days later, I apprehended another evildoer. I was taking a relaxing stroll through the park when I saw a teenage girl bend down and pick up an empty soda can off the grass.

"Halt!" I shouted at her. "Drop that can or I'll start shooting one-liners. You're under arrest!"

"For what?" she asked, acting all innocent.

"Stealing," I announced. "I saw you steal that can. This park is government property, so that can belongs to the government."

"I'm not stealing it, you jerk!" she whined. "I'm picking up litter that someone thoughtlessly threw on the grass."

"Nice alibi," I snorted. "Tell it to the judge."

"You're nuts."

"You'd better put that can back on the grass," I commanded.

"What if I don't?" she challenged me.

"I will tell a joke so funny you will lose control of your bladder. And don't think for a minute I'm bluffing, sister."

She just looked at me, grinning and taunting.

"Okay, you asked for it," I said. "What did Paul Revere say at the end of his famous ride?"

"He said, 'Whoa!'" replied the girl.

"How did you know that?" I asked.

"It's the oldest joke in the book," she said. "Here, take the stupid can. Maybe you can cash it in and get some brains."

She walked away, laughing her head off.

Once again, I had used my superior sense of humor to stop a dangerous criminal from breaking the law. It energized me. It made me feel like a real citizen of Earth. At last, I was making a contribution to society.

I was ready to tackle bigger crimes, bigger criminals. But in my wildest dreams, I never imagined that I was about to save the planet from destruction.

Dream . . .

Chapter 7

HOW TO HANDLE JERKS WHO CALL YOU UP ON THE PHONE AND CLAIM TO BE THE PRESIDENT OF THE UNITED STATES

I know what you're thinking. You've never seen Funny Boy in the newspaper or on TV. There are no Funny Boy action figures or lunch boxes. My dog Punch insists that I'm not real. I'm just a fictional character in a book you're reading. So I must be making all this up, right?

Wrong. **There is a simple reason why the people of Earth don't know about me—there has been a massive cover-up.** That's the truth. The governments of Earth don't want to frighten you citizens. If you knew how close your planet has come to being destroyed, you would panic. No-body would ever believe that the only thing preventing a total takeover of Earth is a kid wearing a yellow tablecloth and a fake nose and glasses.

I suspected the big cover-up when I was watching TV one night with Bob and Punch. The news was on and the anchorman was saying:

"Well, if you loved the movie *E.T.*, we have good news. Hollywood director Steven Spielberg is in Washington, D.C., shooting the sequel, *E.T. Returns with His Big Brother*. Check out this action . . ."

They cut away to show the Washington Monument. Suddenly, an enormous, hideous-looking monster lumbered over to it. The monster wrapped its arms around the Washington Monument and lifted it right out of the ground. People were running away and screaming. Planes were shooting missiles at the monster. It didn't seem to mind. The monster swung the Washington Monument around like a baseball bat. Then it started picking its teeth with it.

"Wow," gushed the anchorman. "We can look forward to *E. T. Returns* sometime this summer."

"Man, I gotta see that!" said Punch.

"Awesome special effects," Bob said.

They *were* awesome special effects, but something about the clip looked fishy to me. It looked too real. I wasn't about to say there actually *was* a monster destroying the Washington Monument, but it sure didn't look like any movie.

Five minutes later the phone rang. Bob picked it up and handed it to me, his face suddenly very serious.

"Who is it?" I asked.

"He says he's the President of the United States."

"Very funny."

I picked up the phone and a man asked, "Is this Silly Boy?"

"Funny Boy," I corrected him. "Who wants to know?"

"It's me," the voice said with some urgency. "The President."

Some people might have been impressed hearing that. But not me. *Anybody* could call me up

and claim to be the President of the United States.

It could have been a phony phone call. I glanced at the clock. It was dinnertime. I felt sure this guy was trying to sell me something.

"Why don't you telemarketers leave us

alone?" I shouted, slamming down the phone.

Two seconds later, the phone rang again.

"What do you want *now*?" I barked into the receiver.

"It's really me," the guy said. "The President."

"Oh yeah?" I said, unimpressed. "Prove it."

"This is important!" the voice shouted. "The fate of the world is at stake!"

"If you're really the President," I said calmly, "you should be able to answer a few simple questions."

"Go ahead," the guy said. "Quickly!"

"What color is the White House?"

"White!"

"Are you in the Oval Office right now?" I asked.

"Yes."

Now I had him. If he was really in the Oval Office—the President's office—there was a simple way to prove it.

"What shape is the room you're in?" I asked.

"Oval!" the guy exclaimed, exasperated.

> I bet he knows who's buried in Grant's Tomb, too.

57

Gosh, I suddenly realized. It really *was* the President! The most powerful man in the world was calling me, Funny Boy, on the telephone. I could hardly believe it. This was the most important, most exciting moment of my life.

It was the moment I had been waiting for ever since I came to Earth. Something pretty important must be going on, or the President wouldn't be calling me. It wasn't some lunatic robbing the library this time. It was something big.

"Mr. President, I am at your service," I said seriously. "Whatever you wish, I will do. My mission is but to serve you and my adopted country. Just say the word."

"I need you to come to Washington right away," the President said.

"I'm kinda busy today," I explained. "I'm doing the laundry and I still have to rake the yard. How about next week?"

"Earth will be *destroyed* next week!" he yelled.

"Oh."

My mind was racing. If Earth was going to be destroyed the next week, I would miss my dentist appointment on Friday. Great, I *hate* going to the dentist! Also, there was no point in raking the yard. If Earth was going to be destroyed next week, the yard wouldn't *be* there anymore.

This is terrific, I thought. I didn't have to do Bob's laundry after all, because if Earth was going to be destroyed, he wouldn't need his clothes. And I wouldn't have to go grocery shopping because we wouldn't be around next week to eat the food because Earth would be destroyed and we'd be dead and—

"I'll be there right away," I told the President.

Chapter 8

HOW TO MAKE THE BEST USE OF YOUR TIME WHEN YOU KNOW THE WORLD WILL BE DESTROYED NEXT THURSDAY

As the taxi pulled up to 1600 Pennsylvania Avenue in Washington, D.C., Bob, Punch, and I were awed by the experience. Here we were, a simple alien from Crouton, his talking dog, and an American factory worker, visiting the White House to meet with the President. Only in America.

"Where's the bathroom?" asked Punch. "I gotta go."

"Fictional characters don't have to use the bathroom," I reminded her.

"Not funny, Funny Boy."

"Just use a tree," Bob suggested.

"I don't use trees," Punch said. Ever since she arrived on Earth and discovered she could talk, Punch decided she was too good to do things that ordinary dogs do.

The three of us walked up to the East Gate, where a uniformed guard was standing at attention.

61

"What are you, a clown?" he said before I had the chance to introduce myself. "The circus isn't due in town for months."

"Hey, who ya callin' a clown?" Punch snapped at the guard. "I'll bite your ear off!"

The guard shrank back in fear.

"I am not a clown. It is I, Funny Boy," I announced. "Earth will be destroyed next week. We have been summoned to save humanity. Didn't you hear about this national emergency?"

"He's really an alien," Bob whispered to the guard. "So's the dog. Their rocket crash-landed into my underwear factory. You've got to believe us."

"I think the three of you are wackos," the guard grumbled.

Wow! It *must* be a real top secret emergency! Even the security forces guarding the White House weren't informed of it.

After a lot of explaining, we finally convinced the guard that we were for real. He ushered us into the White House, where another guard led us down a long corridor.

Suddenly, a lady officer came running over to

us. I thought she was going to arrest me or something.

"Hey! Your dog just pooped on Millard Fillmore's rug!" she said.

"Tell Millard I'll pay for it," Punch barked—I mean *said*.

"Millard Fillmore was the thirteenth President," the guard said. "He's been dead for over one hundred years."

"Then why would he care about his rug?" Punch asked.

We were led into a room with some really fancy chairs and furniture in it. In a few minutes, the President entered.

The President! I'm going to describe him as precisely as I can. He was a tall man, and also rather short. He appeared to be heavier than he looks on television, and thin at the same time. His hair was dark, and also light. His ears were large, on the small side, while his nose was small on the large side.

He was one of those rare men who was tall, short, heavy, thin, with dark and light hair and big and small facial features. There was some-

63

thing familiar about him. Like I met him before. It must be nervousness, I figured. It was awesome to be in the presence of the most powerful man in the world.

"Thank you for coming, Sunny Boy," the President said as we shook hands.

"That's *Funny Boy*, Mr. President. This is my dog, Punchline, and my foster father, Bob Foster."

"We're fictional," Punch announced. I whispered to her to shut up.

The President led us to the Rose Garden, where Punch relieved herself on some roses.

"I understand you use humor to fight evildoers," the President said.

"That's right," I explained. "Once I get them laughing hard enough, they are incapable of carrying out their evil deeds."

"It sounds crazy, but I'm desperate," he sighed, shaking his head sadly. "I've got a global emergency on my hands and the Army can't help. The Navy can't help."

"Why not?" Bob asked.

"They're all getting ready for the big Army-Navy football game this weekend."

"What about the Marines?" Punch asked.

"They're visiting Sea World."

"So you have called on me."

My chest swelled with pride. Only I could save Earth from a threat that was so destructive that the most powerful armed forces in the world were useless.

"I accept the awesome responsibility you have placed before me, Sir. What is my mission?"

"Did you ever hear of Andromeda?"

"Andromeda," I repeated, thinking it over. "Isn't that a medicine people take for constipation?"

WARNING TO READER: If you read the following paragraph, you may actually learn something. If you are reading this book purely for laughs, please—we beg you—*please* do not read the next paragraph!

The President shook his head again sadly. "No. The Great Andromeda Nebula is the nearest galaxy to our own. It is a spiral shape like our own Milky Way, and two million light-years from Earth."

"Ah, yes, now I remember," I said. "And on Crouton, Andromeda is also the name of a popular medicine for constipation."

"An alien creature from Andromeda has invaded our airspace," the President whispered. "It came directly to Washington and immediately vomited on the Lincoln Memorial. Then it ate the National Air and Space Museum. After it was finished, it used the Washington Monument for a toothpick. I had no choice but to meet with the alien. It was a hideous creature. It told me to surrender Earth or it will destroy our entire planet next Thursday."

"Why next Thursday, Mr. President?"

"The alien has several other planets it is scheduled to destroy first. So it had to put us on its waiting list."

I made a mental note to cancel my dentist appointment for next Friday.

"What name does the alien go by?" I asked.

"It didn't say," the President said. "It just said it was hungry, and then it left."

Hmmm. It didn't quite make sense. If a huge alien creature had landed a spaceship in the nation's capital and was causing all this destruction, why wasn't the public going crazy? I would have thought people would be running through the streets screaming their heads off. It would be all over the news.

"I didn't want the public to panic," the President explained. "We told the press that Steven Spielberg is in Washington shooting the sequel to *E.T.—E.T. Returns with His Big Brother*."

"I knew that news report was a fake!" I exclaimed.

"Remember *Jurassic Park*?" the President asked. "Well, that wasn't fictional. Dinosaurs really *did* come back and almost take over. We didn't want anyone to know about it, so we just had Spielberg make a movie about dinosaurs. Luckily, we killed them all before they could take over the planet. The public fell for it. The movie even won some Oscars."

"Very clever," I said. "So whenever there is a national emergency, you just call Hollywood and they make a movie about it so the public doesn't realize how much danger it's really in."

"Exactly. Remember a few years ago when those movies about asteroids hitting Earth came out?"

"Yeah."

"Well," continued the President, "asteroids really *did* hit Earth."

"Really?"

"Have you been to Australia recently?"

"No, why?"

"Don't go. It's not there anymore."

"The asteroid wiped out Australia?" Bob asked, shocked.

"And the Philippines," replied the President. "Thanks to Hollywood, we were able to keep it out of the news."

The President shook his head sadly. "We need help. We have run out of options. Words cannot express the danger Earth is in. This is our nation's darkest hour. The fate of Earth is in your hands now. Good luck, Dummy Boy."

"That's *Funny* Boy."

Chapter 9

THE HIDEOUS PURPLE MONSTER WITH ONE FURRY, DRIPPING EYEBALL

One of the President's aides directed me to a secret location on the outskirts of Washington. It was here that I would meet with the alien and either surrender Earth to it or attempt to defeat it. It was all up to me. It was an awesome responsibility, and I accepted it.

The limo let Bob, Punch, and me out at the front of a stadium. Nobody was around. We walked right through the turnstile and up the ramp until we could see the field.

It was a football field. In the distance, near the 40-yard line, I could see a spaceship. It was the shape of a salami, but enormous. The whole thing reached from one sideline to the other.

And next to the spaceship . . . there it was.

The alien I had seen on TV.

We walked down the row of box seats and hopped the fence to get on the field. As we got closer to the alien, I couldn't believe my eyes. It was a creature about the size of the Statue of Liberty. It was purple. **One hideous-looking furry eyeball was in the middle of its head, which looked like a giant**

misshapen meatball. Goopy fluid was dripping out of the eyeball like runny Jell-O. Its mouth and teeth were enormous.

The alien had six limbs. It was hard to tell which were legs and which were arms. The thing looked like a cross between an insect and a dinosaur.

"D-d-don't worry," Punch stammered. "It's fictional. It can't hurt us."

"I'm scared," Bob said. "Let's just get out of here. How are you gonna make that thing laugh?"

"Relax, Dad," I told him. "Even aliens have a sense of humor. Laughter is the universal language."

"Stop calling me Dad."

As we reached the 10-yard line, I had to cover my nose. The creature was giving off a smell that reminded me of a pair of sweat socks somebody with really stinky feet wore for about a year and then stuffed with rotten eggs, horse manure, and bad cheese.

Not that I ever knew anyone who dressed that way, mind you.

I was trembling with fear. Being funny would take all my power. I stepped forward to the 20-yard line and tried not to show how terrified I was.

"Hey, big guy," I shouted, smiling a big smile. "Don't tell me, you're an alien, right? What a co-incidence! Me, too! It's so nice to meet a fellow visitor from outer—"

The alien let out a roar that rocked me backward. The blast of hot air knocked me off my feet. It swept up my cape and made it wrap around my head so I couldn't see. The stench was unbearable.

"Whoa!" I said. "You could use a Tic-Tac, big guy!"

"WHAT ARE YOU," the alien bellowed, "SOME KIND OF CLOWN?"

"Howdy!" I said cheerily. "I am Funny Boy, defender of Earth, the solar system, the Milky Way galaxy, and ZIP codes so far away even Federal Express doesn't deliver there. What is your name?"

Isn't it weird how aliens always come to Earth and instantly know how to speak English?

"YOU MAY CALL ME MASTER, RULER OF EARTH," the alien bellowed.

"I already have a ruler," I quipped. "I keep it in my desk drawer and use it to measure stuff."

"ARE YOU BEING FACETIOUS?" the alien bellowed.

"Hey, watch your language," I warned. "This is a family-oriented planet. What do they call you on Andromeda?"

"MY NAME IS . . ."—the alien paused for a moment—"BETTY!"

"Betty?" I asked, puzzled. Behind me, I heard Punch giggling.

"BETTY!" bellowed the monster.

"You're kidding, right?" I said. "Usually aliens have names like Blorg or Gigantor or the Slime Thing or something terrifying like that. I never heard of an alien named . . . Betty."

Bob and Punch inched forward. Punch was having a hard time controlling her amusement over the alien's name.

"TELL TOTO TO TONE IT DOWN," Betty thundered, "OR I WILL CRUSH HER LIKE A GRAPE BENEATH MY FEET!"*

*The author defies anyone to find the consecutive letters TOTOTOTO in any other work of literature.

"What am I going to do, Dad?" I whispered to
Bob. "Back on Crouton, my father told me never
to fight with girls."

"Why not?"

"Because they might beat me up."

"I think your father would give you the go-ahead in this case."

I stepped forward to confront Betty. "Why have you come to Earth?" I asked.

"I HAVE COME TO DESTROY YOUR PLANET!"

"What is it with you evil aliens?" I yelled. "You're always in a bad mood when you show up. Right away you want to destroy the planet. Earth is actually a very nice place once you get to know it. Why don't you relax, look around, and see the sights we have to offer on Earth? You'll feel a lot better once you get over your jet lag. Then, if you still have time before you need to go home, *then* you can destroy the planet."

"I WILL DESTROY THIS PLANET WHEN I *CHOOSE* TO . . . ON THURSDAY!"

"And how do you plan to do that, Betty?"

"I AM GOING TO EAT IT."

"Eat it?" That was a new one on me. "How are you going to eat Earth?"

"I WILL START WITH NORTH AMERICA AS

AN APPETIZER. SOUTH AMERICA WILL BE THE FIRST COURSE. THEN I WILL DEVOUR EUROPE. THEN I WILL NIBBLE ON AFRICA. AS A BEVERAGE, I WILL WASH IT ALL DOWN WITH YOUR OCEANS. AND FINALLY, FOR DESSERT, I WILL EAT ASIA. THEN I WILL LET OUT A SATISFYING BURP THAT WILL ECHO ACROSS THE UNIVERSE."

"You forgot Antarctica," Bob pointed out.

"I WILL USE IT TO MAKE ICE CUBES!"

"You should really watch your diet, Betty," I said. "Doctors say it's healthier to eat several small cities over the course of a day rather than to devour an entire continent at once. You don't want to get sick, do you?"

"SILENCE!"

"Believe me, Betty," I said. "Earth tastes awful. I fell down once and got some dirt in my mouth. Yuck! Why don't you eat Venus instead?"

"I ALREADY ATE VENUS!" Betty roared. "IT WAS DELICIOUS."

"Oh."

WARNING TO READER: If you read the following paragraph, you may actually learn something. If you are reading this book purely for laughs, please—we beg you—*please* do not read the next paragraph!

She ate Venus? Venus is a vast wasteland covered by dense clouds of sulfuric acid. The surface temperature is about 750 degrees Fahrenheit.

Compared to Venus, Earth would taste like cotton candy. I had to think of something, and quickly.

"Look," I said. "I'm a reasonable man. I'll make a deal with you. Earthlings are a peace-loving people. Leave now, and they will not attack you with their F-22 fighter jets, hydrogen bombs, and heat-seeking thermonuclear missiles."

"I THOUGHT YOU SAID EARTHLINGS WERE PEACE-LOVING."

"They are," I replied. "Those weapons are only for self-defense."

"EARTH IS 4.5 BILLION YEARS OLD. HAS IT EVER BEEN INVADED?"

"No," I said. "I guess aliens are frightened of all those cool weapons."

"YOU THINK YOU'RE PRETTY FUNNY, DON'T YOU?"

"Yes, I do."

"YOUR WIMPY ATOMIC WEAPONS ARE USELESS AGAINST ME," Betty thundered. "I HAVE BUILT A NUCLEAR SHIELD TO PROTECT MYSELF FROM ATTACK."

"That's not a bad idea," I mused. "We oughta try that."

"TOO LATE. YOU WILL BE CONQUERED. ANDROMEDA WILL RULE THE UNIVERSE!"

"Why did you throw up on the Lincoln Memorial?" I asked. "Was that your way of showing your blatant disregard for our national heroes?"

"NO," Betty explained. "I WAS AIRSICK. I HIT SOME TURBULENCE AS I ENTERED EARTH'S ATMOSPHERE."

"Okay, Betty," I said, walking toward her. "I'm going to ask you nicely one more time. Get back into your spaceship now and take off."

"WHY SHOULD I?"

"Because this is a no-parking zone. If you don't move, the Washington police will tow away your ship and make you pay to get it back."

"PREPOSTEROUS! I REFUSE TO PAY!"

"What's the matter?" Punch asked. "Did you leave your purse home?"

Betty swiveled her head around, flinging a gooey glop of something that hit Punch right in the face. Punch whimpered and scurried away.

"That's it!" I said, rolling up my sleeves. "It's one thing to destroy Earth. But nobody messes with my dog. This is war!"

"WHAT WEAPONS DO YOU HAVE TO FIGHT ME?"

"My weapon is the power of humor," I said. "Jokes. Puns. Quips. Snappy one-liners. I will now demonstrate my superpower of humor. It will cause you to laugh so hard that you will be unable to perform your evil deeds. Helpless with laughter, you will retreat to your spaceship and leave the good people of Earth alone."

"HA! HA! HA!" Betty roared. "DON'T MAKE ME LAUGH!"

"**Well, I**'m going to try. I will now tell a joke **that is so** funny, you will probably die laughing. Ready? Here it is: I went to the doctor and told him I didn't feel well. He told me to drink apple juice after a hot bath. An hour later he called me and asked, 'Did you drink the apple juice?' I said, 'Not yet, I'm still drinking the hot bath!'"

Betty stared at me silently.

"So . . . you don't go for doctor jokes much, eh?" I asked.

Actually, I kind of like that one.

Betty continued to stare at me.

"I know you're out there," I said. "I can hear your eyeballs dripping."

"WHEN ARE YOU GOING TO TELL THE JOKE?" Betty boomed.

I realized I was in trouble. *Big* trouble. If Betty had any sense of humor, it was almost undetectable. I felt sweat gathering on my forehead.

"Okay, how about this one," I said, scrambling to come up with another joke. "A guy walks into a clothing store. 'I'd like to try on those pants in the window,' he tells the salesclerk. The clerk replies, 'Sir, we would prefer you use the dressing room.'"

Betty stared at me without cracking a smile. My jokes were bombing.

"YOU SHOULD CALL YOURSELF UNFUNNY BOY."

I turned around to see if Bob or Punch could help. Bob stepped forward and faced Betty.

"Why did you come here?" he asked. "Earthlings have never bothered you."

"I SAW ALL THOSE SATELLITE DISHES ON YOUR ROOFS."

"So?"

"I WANTED TO SEE WHAT WAS ON."

"You traveled all those light-years just to watch TV?" Bob asked.

"I LOVE TV," Betty replied. "AND THERE

WAS NOTHING ON BUT BAD SITCOMS AND STUPID COMMERCIALS. THAT IS WHY I DE-CIDED TO DESTROY YOUR PLANET."

"Couldn't you just rent a video instead?"

"SHUT UP, EARTH MAN! I WILL TAKE YOUR PATHETIC PLANET, CHOP IT INTO MILLIONS OF PIECES, AND SPRINKLE IT ON MY SALAD!"

The thought of a planet being sprinkled onto a salad reminded me of Crouton. I thought back to my childhood there. My old school. The old field where I used to play ball. The old lake where I used to swim.

Man, I hated Crouton! Just thinking about it made tears well up in my eyes.

"Look, now you made him cry," Bob said to Betty. "Why don't you pick on somebody your own size?"

"THERE *IS* NOBODY MY SIZE!"

"There would be if you didn't eat so much," Bob retorted.

"If you're so hungry, why don't you eat the moon?" Punch suggested. "They say it's made of cheese."

"ENOUGH BAD JOKES! I MUST LEAVE NOW."

"Aha!" I said, drying my eyes. "The power of our barbs and quips has caused you to retreat to Andromeda! I knew I would defeat you."

"NO," Betty said. "MY FAVORITE TV SHOW BACK HOME IS ON—*ANDROMEDA'S FUNNIEST HOME VIDEOS*. I WILL BE BACK NEXT THURSDAY. MEET ME AT THE WHITE HOUSE, WHERE I WILL BEGIN THE DESTRUCTION OF YOUR PLANET."

"I'll be there," I said defiantly.

"WITH FUNNIER JOKES, I HOPE."

"So funny you'll forget to laugh."

"YOU REMIND ME OF A CALENDAR, FUNNY BOY."

"Why is that?"

"YOUR DAYS ARE NUMBERED."

Chapter 10

PUTTING ON PAJAMAS RIGHT AFTER YOU TAKE THEM OUT OF THE DRYER (AND OTHER JOYS OF LIVING ON EARTH)

After my confrontation with Betty, I tried to contact the President. Unfortunately, he was in hiding. It would be up to Bob, Punch, and me to save Earth.

As I thought about the end of the world, I remembered all the good things I had experienced on your planet since I arrived here.

SUGGESTION TO READER: As you read the following, have a friend hum *America the Beautiful* in the background.

Microwave popcorn, for example. And Play-Doh. Putting on a pair of pajamas right after you take them out of the dryer. It's the best feeling in the world.

Electronic mail. Gravity. Where would we be without gravity? Floating all over the place. Chocolate. Velcro. Wiffle balls. Free samples. Nintendo.

Lemonade on a hot day. Hot chocolate on a cold one. Hey, how come when you're drinking hot chocolate the marshmallows float away from your mouth, but when you're drinking lemonade the ice cubes float *into* your mouth? That's what I want to know.

Those boxes of tissues where the next tissue pops up automatically when you pull out the tissue above it.

Self-flushing toilets. How do they know when you're done?

And thermos bottles. How do they know to keep cold things cold and hot things hot?

Remote controls. Isn't it hard to believe there was a time when people actually had to get up and change the channel on the set? How did they survive?

Strip malls! The Home Shopping Network! Frisbees!

Don't forget fire hydrants!

Was I going to let some intergalactic jerk take all those things away from us? No way!

If I let some alien creep have her way, she would blow us off the face of the planet. And there would be other alien creeps threatening other planets. They would turn every inhabitable planet into a barren, empty nothingness covered by trees and grass and water—pretty much what Earth was like before humans showed up and put a McDonald's on every other block. I couldn't let that happen. But what was I going to do about it?

I had to come up with some killer jokes by Thursday, or Earth was doomed.

So, how are you enjoying the story so far? Do you think Earth is doomed, or will Funny Boy come up with some better jokes and save the planet? Will he ever realize he's a fictional character? More importantly, will he ever realize how bad his jokes are? Will Bob be able to convince the *National Inspirer* that he found a real alien so he can collect the million-dollar reward? Will Betty go on Weight Watchers? And will Punch ever be potty-trained? Keep reading and find out!

Chapter 11

BEING A FICTIONAL CHARACTER IS REALLY THE PITS

Bob, Punch, and I rushed to the Library of Congress on Independence Avenue, where they have a copy of every book ever printed. We borrowed the jokebooks, all 5,324 of them. The three of us went through them one by one. We must have read a trillion jokes. Carefully, we weeded out all the unfunny ones.

I was extremely nervous about meeting up with Betty again. I tried to hide it, but I guess it showed.

"Will you calm down?" Punch asked me. "Don't you realize you're fictional? There's going to be a happy ending. I promise you."

"How many times do I have to tell you? I'm not fictional! I'm real."

"Yeah, right."

"You think I'm fictional, eh?" I asked. "Well, can a fictional character do *this*?"

I crossed my eyes, stuck out my tongue and touched my nose, patted my head, and rubbed my belly in circles.

"*Only* fictional characters can do that," Punch insisted. "Besides, you didn't actually *do* it. It was just words on a page. You only did it in the reader's imagination. It didn't really happen."

I began to feel extremely depressed. What if Punch was right? What if I really was only a fictional character? What would be the point of doing *anything*? What was the point in saving Earth from evildoers? I might as well just sit around and do nothing.

So that's what I did. I sat there and did nothing. I just sat. Let somebody else save the world, I decided. It's not my responsibility. I started tapping my fingers on the desk and humming to myself.

Man, it was boring! It felt bad enough that I

might be fictional. But being *bored* and fictional was really the pits.

Fictional or not, I had to act, and act now. If I didn't save the world, some other fictional super-hero might come along and get all the credit. I couldn't have that.

There was an Internet workstation in the library, so we logged on and checked out every Web site that had jokes on it. We selected the funniest ones and I memorized them. By Thursday, we were armed with enough jokes to crack up the most humorless of all villains. We rushed back to the White House for one final confrontation with Betty.

Isn't this exciting?

Chapter 12

YOU HAVE FAILED
TO MAKE ME LAUGH.
NOW YOU MUST DIE.

"Make way!" I said, pushing past the crowds gathered at the East Gate of the White House. "It is I, Funny Boy. I am here to save your world."

When we reached the front, a security guard stuck his arm up in front of me.

"Sorry, buddy," he said. "This area is sealed off today."

"Why?" I asked.

"There's a movie crew here. They're shooting the sequel to *E. T.*"

Bob shoved the guard aside. "When are you people going to get it?" he shouted. "This is no movie! Earth is being invaded by a real alien! And we're the only ones who can stop her!"

"Real alien?" chuckled the guard. "Man, you are a nutcase. Everybody knows aliens don't exist."

Looking over the guard's shoulder, I could see Betty on the White House lawn. And she clearly wasn't there for the annual Easter egg roll. She was drooling and snorting and looking very menacing.

"IT'S ABOUT TIME YOU WIMPS SHOWED UP!" she said when she saw us. We rushed past the guard. "TODAY IS THE GLORIOUS DAY EARTH WILL BE DESTROYED! AND I'M FEELING HUNGRY!"

"No, today is the day *you* will be destroyed, Betty!" I insisted. "Destroyed by the power of wit and humor."

"YOU COULDN'T MAKE ME LAUGH IF YOUR LIFE DEPENDED ON IT!" Betty roared. "AND BY THE WAY, YOUR LIFE *DOES* DEPEND ON IT."

"Oh yeah?" I said. "Listen to this!—An eight-year-old boy hadn't spoken in his entire life. Then one day, as his family sat down to breakfast, he suddenly asked, 'Where's the cream cheese?' Everyone was shocked. When they recovered,

they all asked him why he had never spoken before. 'Well,' he said, 'up until now we've always
had cream cheese.'"

"UGH. THE LAST TIME I HEARD THAT JOKE,"
Betty groaned, "MOUNT RUSHMORE HAD THREE
HEADS."

I was not discouraged. I was just warming up,
softening her up for my best jokes.

"Where was the Declaration of Independence
signed?" I asked.

"WHERE?" Betty responded.

"On the bottom!"

Nothing. No response at all. If I could just
make her laugh a little, I reasoned, I would hit her
with my best jokes and she would be unable to
eat *anything*, much less the entire planet.

"YOUR MINDLESS JOKES HAVE BECOME
TIRESOME," Betty said, grabbing me by the
arms. "IT IS TIME YOUR MISERABLE LIFE CAME
TO AN END. AND EARTH WITH IT!"

"Go ahead and kill him," Punch said. "He's fictional anyway."

"Wait!" I begged. "I have lots more jokes to
tell you!"

"ENOUGH JOKES!" Betty roared. "IT IS TIME FOR THE EATING TO BEGIN!"

Betty picked up a bowl and put it on the ground in front of me.

"IT WOULD NOT BE POLITE FOR ME TO EAT ALONE," she said. "WON'T YOU JOIN ME IN YOUR LAST MEAL, FUNNY BOY?"

"Croutons!" I exclaimed, looking in the bowl.

"NOT JUST CROUTONS," Betty sneered. "CROUTONITE!"

Croutonite! Little chunks of my home planet. They had been placed in my rocket ship before it was launched to Earth. How did Betty get them? Suddenly, I felt funny. Or, I should say, I didn't feel funny at all.

"THE CROUTONITE IS SAPPING YOUR POWERS, FUNNY BOY. YOU ARE LOSING YOUR SENSE OF HUMOR!"

I thought that happened on Page 1.

She was right! For the first time in my life, I saw no humor at all in the situation.

"Without my sense of humor," I moaned, "I'll die!"

"THAT'S RIGHT, FUNNY BOY! AND I WILL RULE THE UNIVERSE! HAHAHAHAHA!"

"You're a sick, sick alien!"

"DO NOT FEEL SO BAD, FUNNY BOY," Betty said, "YOU WERE NEVER THAT FUNNY TO BEGIN WITH. PERHAPS YOU HAVE ONE LAST REQUEST BEFORE YOU DIE?"

"Yes," I groaned. "My last request is that you don't kill me."

"THAT WAS YOUR LAST JOKE, FUNNY BOY," Betty said. "PATHETIC AS IT WAS."

I could feel my sense of humor slipping away. I tried to think of why the chicken crossed the road. I didn't have a clue. I couldn't come up with the reason why firemen wear red suspenders. I had no idea why anyone would throw a clock out a window. Nothing was funny to me anymore.

"Don't give in!" Bob yelled. "Try telling a joke, Funny Boy!"

"This walrus walks into a dentist's office," I groaned, straining to remember the rest. "And he says to the dentist . . . uh . . . I forgot. I'm too weak. Too weak . . ."

"YOU ARE HELPLESS BEFORE ME," Betty boomed. "I DO NOT HAVE TO HEAR YOUR LAME ATTEMPTS AT HUMOR ANYMORE. NOW I MUST BEGIN TO EAT EARTH!"

"Don't give up now, Funny Boy!" Punch begged. "You're our only hope!"

"I'm too weak, Punch!" I moaned. "I can't think of my jokes!"

"How about riddles?" she said. "Maybe they would work."

"Too weak . . . don't remember the punch lines . . ."

"*I'll* say the punch lines!" Punch announced proudly.

"You?"

It almost made me laugh. Punch never had a sense of humor. She's so unfunny, she couldn't make a hyena laugh.

"Let me try," Punch begged. "I've memorized all your jokes. We have nothing to lose at this point. If we don't try something, we'll all die!"

It's about time he gave me a few lines.

"Okay," I muttered desperately. "I'll say the riddle and you say the punch line."

"Hey, Betty!" shouted Punch. "Before you start eating, Funny Boy and I would like to have a word with you."

Betty waddled over to us. Punch motioned for me to start.

"How long is the longest finger in the world?" I managed to grunt through my pain.

"I DO NOT KNOW."

"Eleven inches," Punch replied. "If it were twelve inches, it would be a foot."

Betty just stared at us with a puzzled expression on her face. Punch motioned for me to try another one.

"A penny and a dollar were on top of the Empire State Building," I said. "The penny jumped off. Why didn't the dollar?"

"It had more sense," Punch replied.

Betty didn't crack a smile. She sure was a tough audience.

"Which travels faster, heat or cold?" I asked.

101

"Heat," Punch replied. "It's easy to catch cold."

"THAT WAS SO FUNNY I FORGOT TO LAUGH," Betty roared.

"Why does corn think farmers are disgusting?" I asked.

"Because they pick their ears," Punch replied immediately. Punch was right. She *did* know all my jokes.

"YOU NEED SOME NEW JOKE WRITERS," Betty said. "THE LAST TIME I HEARD THAT, I FELL OFF MY DINOSAUR."

"What's the difference between a fish and a piano?" I asked.

"You can't tune a fish," Punch said. "Get it? Tune a fish? Tuna fish?"

"TOTALLY UNFUNNY. NOW YOU MUST DIE!"

"Wait!" I pleaded. "What animal eats with its tail?"

"They all do," Punch replied. "It's not like they can take them off!"

"PLEASE SHUT UP," Betty moaned. "YOU'RE NOT AT ALL FUNNY."

"Did you know it takes three sheep to make a

sweater?" I asked.

"I didn't even know sheep could knit," Punch replied.

"SHUT UP!" Betty moaned, holding her ears. "PLEASE SHUT UP."

"What animal can jump higher than a house?" I asked.

"All of them," Punch said. "Houses can't jump."

"STOP!" Betty moaned. "CAN'T YOU SEE HOW NOT FUNNY YOU ARE?"

"What would you do if you broke your arm in two places?" I asked.

"I wouldn't go back to those two places anymore," Punch replied.

"I'M GETTING A MIGRAINE," Betty moaned, holding her enormous head.

"If you go to the bathroom in France," I asked, "what are you?"

"You're a peein'!" Punch said. "Get it, European?"

"OH, THE PAIN . . . THE PAIN . . ."

Seeing an opportunity, Bob rushed forward. He grabbed the bowl of Croutonite and took it

away. Almost instantly, I started feeling funny again.

Betty was holding the sides of her head and stumbling around like a wounded animal. I felt a little bad, lowering myself to toilet humor. But, hey, the world was at stake. You gotta do what you gotta do.

"You doubted the power of my amazing sense of humor!" I shouted at Betty. "And look at you now. You're a pathetic mass of glop. My powers are back. Now I will tell jokes so funny you'll die laughing."

"SHUT UP! PLEASE, I'M BEGGING YOU! STOP TELLING YOUR STUPID JOKES!"

Suddenly, Betty gasped for breath, then toppled over with a thud. Her eyes rolled up. There was silence.

"She's . . . dead!" Punch exclaimed. "You killed her."

It was true. Betty lay there on the White House lawn without moving.

" 'Twas humor that killed the beast," I said softly.

"I guess those riddles were so bad, she

couldn't stand it anymore," Punch said.

"I'd almost rather be dead than have to listen to you two trying to be funny," one of the White House security guards added.

"Some folks," I announced solemnly, "just can't take a joke."

Chapter 13

THE BIG SURPRISE ENDING THAT WILL COMPLETELY SHOCK YOU, UNLESS YOU ALREADY GUESSED IT

"They've *got* to believe *this* alien story!" Bob said excitedly. "The thing died right on the White House lawn! I can collect the reward from the *National Inspirer*. I'll be rich, rich, *rich*!"

At that moment, a man with a beard rushed over. I recognized his face right away. It was Steven Spielberg.

"Cut!" he shouted. "That was beautiful! Print it! Take five, everybody!"

"What are *you* doing here?" I asked Spielberg.

"What do you think?" Spielberg asked. "I'm shooting *E.T. Returns*. You were terrific! Such drama! Such emotion! You might win the Oscar for best actor!"

"But the President told me the alien was real. He said you were only shooting a movie so the public wouldn't find out—"

"Now the public will find out the *truth*!" shouted a voice behind us.

"Who said that?" asked Spielberg.

"I did."

The voice was coming from inside Betty's spaceship. It was familiar to me, somehow. We all turned around. Spielberg ordered his crew to quickly turn on their cameras and start filming.

A small figure emerged from the shadows of Betty's spaceship.

"Bronk!" I shouted.

"Bronk?" Bob asked. "Who's Bronk?"

"My little brother," I replied.

"That's right!" Bronk said with a sneer. "It's me. Your stinking little brother who you loved to torture so much back home on Crouton. You thought you'd seen the last of me. Not quite, Funny Boy. After Mom and Dad sent you away, I realized something was missing in my

life—revenge! I never had the chance to get
back at you for those spitballs you shot at me.
So I got a spaceship of my own, stopped off at
Andromeda to hire Betty, and brought her here
to destroy Earth . . . with *you* on it."

"Well, your plan didn't work," I told Bronk.
"Betty's dead."

"That's okay," Bronk said as he reached into his pocket. "I'm still going to get my revenge."

"He's going for a gun!" Bob shouted. Everyone dove for cover.

Bronk didn't pull out a gun. He pulled out a straw. Then he wadded up a piece of paper and put it in his mouth. And then he put the straw to his lips and shot a spitball right at my fore-head.

"Ha!" Bronk said triumphantly. "I finally got you back."

"You're sick, Bronk," I said. "Really sick."

"Cut!" shouted Steven Spielberg. "Beautiful! What an ending! Academy Awards, here I come!"

What an ending, indeed. When the story reached the front pages of all the newspapers the next day, I became an international celebrity superhero known the world over as Funny Boy. Steven Spielberg offered me ten million dollars for the movie rights to my life story. I gave a million dollars to Bob, and as a retirement present, his employer gave him a lifetime supply of underwear. Bronk was sent back to Crouton.

So Punch was right about one thing—we *did* have a happy ending. After it was all over, she became the first dog in history to have her own talk show.

Well, my work is done here. You have turned the

pages. I have used the forces of funniness to thwart evil. Together, we have made the world safe. Safe for remote-control cars that don't steer. Safe for infomercials for gizmos that don't make you lose weight. Safe for Kraft Macaroni and Cheese and roller hockey and the Cartoon Network.

Until we meet again, my friends, I leave you with one small piece of advice. Always remember my slogan: laughter is the best medicine. But if you fall off a bridge or something, don't sit there laughing like an idiot. Call an ambulance.

Ha! Ha! Ha!

I better be careful. I'm going to laugh one of my heads off.

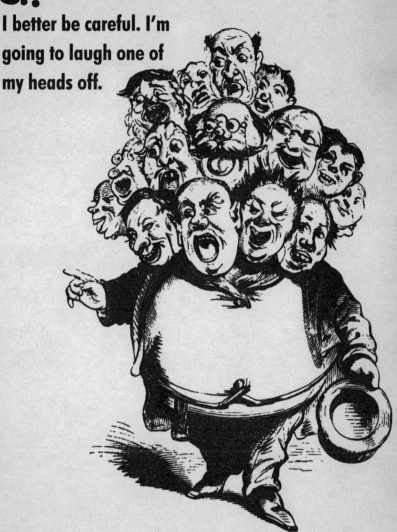

Still, I sure wish there were more stories about Funny Boy. . . .

Your prayers have been answered!
Funny Boy is coming back at you in . . .

Available in any decent bookstore
in June 2000!

**To help sustain your interest in fine literature,
we are proud to publish these other L. A. F.:) books:**

(Okay, you got your $3.99 worth. Go out and buy another L. A. F:) book.)